We Learn All About Community Helpers

A Complete Resource
for Preschool, Kindergarten,
and First Grade Teachers

by Sharon MacDonald

Fearon Teacher Aids
Belmont, California

Illustrator: Pauline Phung

Entire contents copyright © 1988 by Fearon Teacher Aids,
500 Harbor Boulevard, Belmont, California 94002.
Permission is hereby granted to reproduce the materials
in this book for noncommercial classroom use.

ISBN 0-8224-4599-9

Printed in the United States of America

1. 9 8

Contents

1 To the Teacher

TEACHER'S GUIDE 3–16

    4   About Community Helpers
    5   Police Officers
    9   Fire Fighters
  11   Post Office Workers
  14   Dentists
  16   Suggested Reading

STUDENT WORKSHEETS 17–32

PATTERN PAGES 33–43

  35   Community-Helper Book Patterns
  41   Community-Helper Patterns

To the Teacher

Dear Teacher:

In this book you will find everything you need to introduce the community helpers into your classroom. It is a complete unit packed full of background information and learning activities that will help you teach children about community helpers.

The materials are presented in five sections—About Community Helpers, Police Officers, Fire Fighters, Post Office Workers, and Dentists. You can pick and choose which topics you want to use. Each section contains an *introduction* and *activities*. The introductions give the basics of the topics, so there is little need for you to gather additional information on community helpers. The activities suggest projects for art time, snack time, play time, and learning time that correspond to and reinforce the topics. Since there are a number of activities listed for each topic, you can choose the ones that are appropriate for your class's skill level.

The *suggested reading* at the end of the teacher's guide lists reading and picture books that will enhance the children's enjoyment of community helpers. I suggest that when you introduce a topic, you also read one or two of the books to the children. You could also leave out picture books for the children to look at on their own.

The fourteen reproducible *worksheets* incorporate thinking and concept skills such as visual-discrimination skills and the fine-motor skills of coloring, drawing, cutting, and pasting. Suggestions for using the worksheets and the nine reproducible *pattern pages* are included with the activities.

Have fun bringing community helpers to your classroom!

Sincerely,

Sharon MacDonald

TEACHER'S GUIDE

About Community Helpers

INTRODUCTION

A *community* is a group of people living in the same place. A neighborhood, a town, or a city can be a community. A *community helper* is someone who does a job that helps the community.

There are many different types of community helpers. Some help keep us safe, such as police officers and fire fighters. Some help keep us healthy, such as doctors and dentists. Teachers help us learn, garbage collectors help keep our community clean, letter carriers help us communicate, and store clerks help us when we need to buy things. People who work as bus drivers, lawyers, barbers, veterinarians, and secretaries are also community helpers.

ACTIVITIES

▶ Duplicate and hand out Worksheet 1 (page 19). Have the children do the following things:
1. Using a pencil, draw a line from the house to the park. (Make sure you stay on the road.) Draw a ball next to the swings.
2. Follow the road from the park to the grocery store. Circle the apple.
3. Follow the road from the grocery store to the gas station. Color the sign yellow.
4. Follow the road from the gas station to the bank. Draw a dollar (a rectangle) above the bank.
5. Follow the road from the bank to the post office. Draw a letter (a rectangle) next to the flag.
6. Follow the road from the post office to the school. Color the trees green.
7. Follow the road from the school to the restaurant. Draw a pizza (a circle) near the restaurant.
8. Follow the road from the restaurant to the house. Color the roof red.

About Community Helpers

ACTIVITIES

- If possible, take a walk or a bus ride around the community. Point out different community helpers and the places they work.

- Obtain a city, town, or neighborhood map. Help the children find the school, fire station, and police station on the map.

- Use the patterns on pages 41–43 to make community-helper flannel-board cutouts. Trace and cut out different community helpers. Glue to the back of a piece of sandpaper. Cut out the figures. Use the pieces to make up a community-helper flannel-board story.

- Have children tell stories about what they would like to be when they grow up.

Police Officers

INTRODUCTION

Police officers serve the community in many ways. They help enforce laws and maintain order. They guard against crime, direct traffic to keep it running smoothly, help accident victims, and find lost persons. The police also investigate crimes and arrest lawbreakers.

There are several different types of police officers. Each type has special things to do. *Patrol officers* are given certain areas to watch. They patrol these areas on foot, in squad cars, or on motorcycles. Some patrol officers use horses to watch parks and beaches. While

Police Officers

patrolling, the police look for anything that might hurt people or property. Sometimes patrol officers are given orders to go to places where there is trouble. *Traffic officers* help keep streets and highways safe. They enforce safety laws for motor vehicles and find out who is responsible for traffic accidents. They also direct traffic, protect pedestrians, and enforce parking laws. Some police departments use helicopters to watch the traffic from the air. *Detectives* investigate crimes such as robbery and murder.

The police have tools that help them with their work. All police officers have badges so people will know who they are. Most police officers carry two-way pocket radios so they can keep in touch with the police station. They also carry handcuffs in case they have to arrest a criminal. Traffic officers have whistles to help them direct traffic. Patrol officers use special police cars or motorcycles that have red lights and sirens. These let people know they should move out of the way of the police vehicle. The cars and motorcycles also have two-way radios so the officers can get assignments and backup help.

Police officers work eight hours a day. They begin their day with roll call. During roll call, the officers' sergeant or captain gives them the day's instructions, information on wanted criminals, and other information that helps the officers while they are on duty.

ACTIVITIES

- ▶ Make a safety-rule bulletin board. Use pictures of different street signs, the emergency number for your area, and banners with safety rules such as "Cross the street at the corner or at a crosswalk," "Never talk to strangers," "Use hand signals when riding your bike," and "Don't play with guns or knives."

- ▶ If possible, have a police officer talk to your class about his or her work.

- ▶ Have children learn their phone numbers and street addresses.

Police Officers

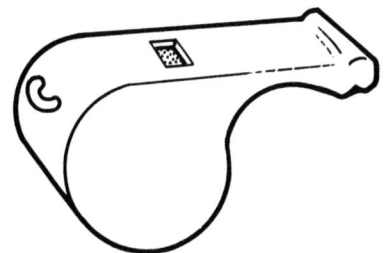

ACTIVITIES

▶ Teach children the correct hand signals. If possible, obtain a tricycle and let children ride it using the hand signals.

▶ Duplicate and hand out Worksheet 2 (page 20). Have the children color only the objects a police officer might use.

▶ Play a police-officer game. Have the children sit in a circle. Choose one child to be a parent and another to be a police officer. Have the parent tell the officer that the parent's child is lost. The parent should describe another child in the class to the police officer. From the description, the officer must identify who the lost child is. Give each child a chance to be a parent or a police officer.

▶ Teach the children how to draw police whistles. Draw the following on a chalkboard:

1. Draw a circle.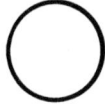

2. Add another circle.

3. Add another circle.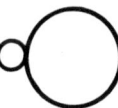

4. Add part of a rectangle.

5. Add another rectangle.

Let the children make their own whistles on pieces of paper.

Police Officers

ACTIVITIES

▶ Duplicate and hand out Worksheet 3 (page 21). Have the children color the stop sign red. Then have them cut out the letters at the bottom of the page and glue them to the stop sign to make the word *stop*.

▶ Give the children pieces of foil, construction paper, and glue. Let them make their own police badges.

▶ Duplicate and hand out Worksheet 4 (page 22). Have the children color-by-number to find the hidden traffic light.

▶ Have the children make community-helper books. Duplicate the book patterns on pages 35–40. Have the children color the pictures and trace the words. When they are finished, staple the pages inside a folded piece of construction paper. Write "My Community-Helper Book" and the child's name on the cover.

▶ Teach the children how to draw traffic lights. Draw the following on a chalkboard:

1. Draw a rectangle.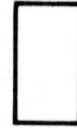

2. Add three circles.

3. Add a triangle.

Let the children make their own traffic lights on pieces of paper.

8

Fire Fighters

INTRODUCTION

Fire fighters have very important jobs. They risk their lives to save people and protect property from fires. Fire fighters also rescue people who are trapped in cars or trains after accidents, help people when there are disasters such as floods and earthquakes, and teach fire safety.

Fire fighters have to go to school to learn things such as ways to prevent and fight fires, what to look for when a building is inspected for fire hazards, and first aid. Fire fighters also learn how to handle the special tools and equipment they use in their job.

When they hear that a fire has broken out, the fire department headquarters notifies the closest fire station. There are always fire fighters on duty at a fire station. The fire trucks are always ready to go. Some of the fire fighters sleep in the firehouse. When there is a fire late at night, the fire fighters are dressed in less than a minute. They slide down a pole to a waiting truck. Once the fire fighters arrive at the fire, they use two-way radios to tell headquarters how serious the fire is. Sometimes they ask for more help.

Fire fighters use a lot of different equipment to fight fires. They have several different types of fire trucks. Some trucks are called *pumpers*. These trucks have large pumps that take water from a fire hydrant and pump it through hoses that attach to the truck. *Ladder trucks* have ladders that can be raised as high as 100 feet (30 meters). Some ladder trucks have elevating platforms that can hold several people. These trucks help fire fighters rescue people from the tops of buildings. Ladder trucks are so big they have to be steered by two people.

All the fire trucks carry special equipment. Usually a pumper has a water tank, different-size hoses, fire axes, and fire extinguishers. Some pumpers also carry tools such as shovels and rakes to help put out outdoor fires. Ladder trucks have portable ladders, stretchers, and first-aid kits. They also carry tools that help the fire fighters open or break into buildings or rooms so hot air and smoke can escape. These tools include axes, power saws, and sledgehammers. Between fires, fire fighters must clean every piece of their equipment so the equipment will work perfectly at the next fire.

Fire fighters have to wear clothes that protect them against flames, falling objects, and other hazards. They have coats that come down to their knees and are made of a heavy material that protects the fire fighters from heat. They also wear specially made pants, shirts, boots, and gloves. Fire fighters' helmets have a long brim that keeps ashes from falling down the fire fighters' necks. Fire fighters also use gas masks and air tanks so they don't breathe in smoke and poisonous gases.

Fire Fighters

ACTIVITIES

▶ Have children discuss what they would do in an emergency situation such as a fire. Tell them ways to prevent fires and give practical advice about what to do in emergencies.

▶ Arrange a tour of a fire station. Point out the different equipment the fire fighters use.

▶ Obtain toy models of different safety vehicles—fire trucks, ambulances, police cars. Let the children play with the cars and make up stories about rescue missions.

▶ Duplicate and hand out Worksheet 5 (page 23). Have the children complete the pattern in each row using the cards at the bottom of the worksheet.

▶ Duplicate and hand out Worksheet 6 (page 24). Have the children connect the dots from 1 to 25 to complete the fire truck.

▶ Make fire-fighter finger puppets. Use the pattern below to cut out ovals from red construction paper. Cut a semicircle in each oval as shown. Glue a white square on the semicircle and fold the semicircle up. Write a number on the square. Place the puppets over children's fingers and draw on faces. Let the children put on a puppet show!

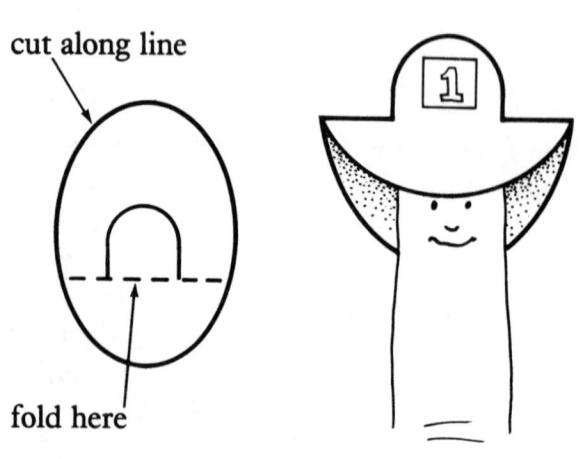

fire helmet pattern

▶ Duplicate and hand out Worksheet 7 (page 25). Have the children color the objects that are the same in each row.

Fire Fighters

ACTIVITIES

▶ Have the children make fire hydrants. Obtain an empty thread spool for each child. Let the children paint the spools red.

▶ Duplicate and hand out Worksheet 8 (page 26). Have the children cut and then paste the cards so they form a fire story.

▶ Duplicate and hand out Worksheet 9 (page 27). Have the children find the path through the maze.

▶ Hand out precut circular and rectangular shapes. Let the children glue the shapes on construction paper to make fire trucks. They can use crayons to add details.

Post Office Workers

INTRODUCTION

A post office is a place that handles mail. The post office sends and delivers mail to people. Most post offices also sell stamps and other postal materials. United States post offices handle more than 110 billion pieces of mail a year.

There are many different types of jobs in a post office. Postal workers called *mail handlers* pick up letters and packages from mailboxes and take them to a nearby post office. They usually collect mail from the mailboxes several times a day.

Once the mail reaches the post office, *postal clerks* sort the letters. The postal clerks use several different machines that help them do their work. Once the mail has been sorted, *letter carriers* take the mail and deliver it. They arrange the mail in the order it will be delivered by putting it into special cases that have slots for each address.

11

Post Office Workers

Each letter carrier has a particular area in which to deliver mail. These areas are called the letter carriers' routes. Many letter carriers walk their routes, though some drive cars or special post office vehicles. As a letter carrier delivers the mail, he or she also picks up any outgoing mail left in the personal mailboxes along the route. The letter carrier delivers this mail to the post office.

There are many machines in a post office. When postal clerks sort the mail they place the mail on a moving belt. The belt moves the mail to a machine called an *edger-feeder*. The edger-feeder sorts the mail by envelope size. When the mail has been sorted by size it moves to another machine called a *facer-canceler*. This machine senses where the stamp is on the envelope and cancels the stamp by putting a black mark over it so it cannot be used again. The machine also puts

a *postmark* on the envelope. The postmark tells the date, the name of the post office, the state, and the ZIP code for the area.

A machine called a *ZIP mail translator* sorts the postmarked letters according to destination. Postal clerks push buttons on the machine to send each letter into the correct holding bin for its destination. Once the letters have been sorted, they are bundled and put into mailbags. The letters will then be taken by truck or plane to the post offices closest to their destinations.

ACTIVITIES

▶ Duplicate and hand out Worksheet 10 (page 28). Have the children connect the dots from A to Z to complete the mailbox.

▶ Let the children pretend to be letter carriers. Supply them with an old purse or tote bag, a "letter carrier" hat, and some junk mail. Let the children take turns delivering mail.

▶ Duplicate and hand out Worksheet 11 (page 29). Have the children trace over the lines to lead each community helper to his or her vehicle.

Post Office Workers

ACTIVITIES

▶ Help the children set up a pretend post office. Use a box with a slit, such as a tissue box, for a mailbox. Supply the children with rubber stamps and junk mail. Let them take turns being postal clerks canceling and sorting mail.

▶ If possible, take the children on a field trip to a post office. Before you go, write short notes or let the class help you draw pictures to send to special people. Have the children observe you as you place the notes in envelopes and address the envelopes. Stress the importance of having ZIP codes on the letters. Purchase stamps at the post office and show the children how to place them on the letters. Let the children drop the letters in the mailbox.

▶ If possible, have a letter carrier come to class and describe his or her job.

▶ Use the patterns on pages 41–43 to make community-helper stencils. Duplicate the patterns, glue them on tagboard, and cut out. Let the children trace around the stencils on pieces of paper.

▶ Have the children make "stamps" out of construction paper. Give each child a rectangular piece of paper. Have the children color the paper with crayons or markers. When the children have finished, cut the paper into small square "stamps." Let the children glue their stamps to envelopes or letters.

▶ Have children decorate graham cracker "stamps" with frosting. Eat at snack time.

13

Post Office Workers

ACTIVITIES

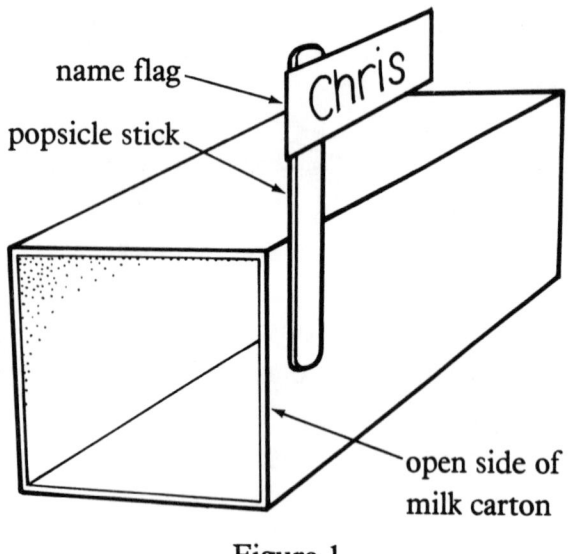

Figure 1

▶ Make milk-carton mailboxes. Cut off the tops of half-gallon milk cartons. Give each child a piece of blue construction paper to decorate. Help the children glue the construction paper around the outside of the milk carton. Then help the children print their names on 2" × 4" pieces of white paper. Glue these pieces of paper to popsicle sticks, and glue the popsicle sticks to the milk cartons. (See Figure 1.) Help the children write letters to put in their mailboxes.

Dentists

INTRODUCTION

Dentists help keep people healthy in many ways. They treat diseases of the teeth and of the mouth. They help straighten people's teeth. Some dentists make replacements for teeth called *dentures*. Others perform operations on the mouth and jaws. Dentists also help prevent disease. They show people how to brush and floss teeth properly. They might tell patients which foods are good to eat and which foods the patients should avoid.

Dentists have to use different types of equipment. They have a *dental chair* that can be adjusted to fit each patient. They also have a *dental unit* which has an instrument table, a cold-water faucet, a small sink, warm water and air sprays, and a *dental engine*. The dental engine looks like a big grasshopper leg and is used for cleaning and drilling teeth.

Dentists use *X-ray machines* to take pictures of people's teeth. These pictures help the dentists find cavities and diseases.

Dentists must go to school for many years to learn how to care for teeth and gums. When they finish school, they receive a diploma that shows they went to school. However, most dentists must continue to learn after they finish school. They do this by attending lectures, reading magazines about dental practices, and talking to other dentists.

Dentists

ACTIVITIES

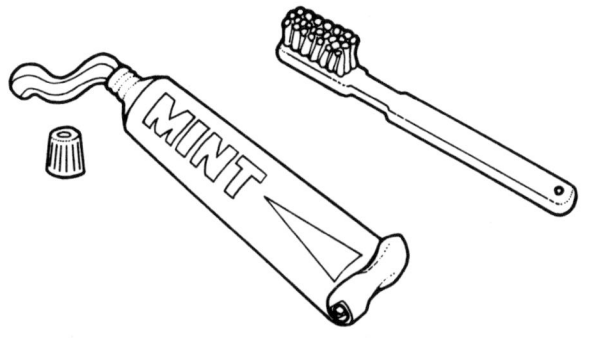

▶ Teach children how to brush and floss their teeth properly.

▶ Duplicate and hand out Worksheet 12 (page 30). Have the children cut out each tool card and paste it next to the community helper who uses that tool.

▶ Duplicate and hand out Worksheet 13 (page 31). Have the children color the objects that are the same in each row.

▶ Duplicate and hand out Worksheet 14 (page 32). Have the children find the community helper that is different in each row.

▶ If possible, bring in some dental tools and some dentures to show children.

▶ Ask children to tell about experiences they have had at a dentist's office.

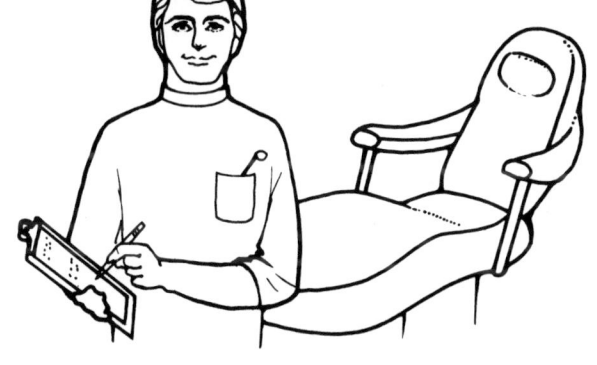

▶ Let children draw pictures of teeth on pieces of paper.

▶ Play a job-hat game. Draw different helpers' hats on index cards (one hat per card). Place the cards in a box. Have a child choose a card and then act out the job implied by the picture on the card. The rest of the class has to guess which helper the child is imitating. The child who guesses correctly gets to draw the next card.

▶ Have children eat snacks that are good for their teeth, such as apples or carrots.

Suggested Reading

Averill, Esther. *The Fire Cat*. New York: Harper & Row, 1983. (K-3).

Brown, Margaret W. *The Little Fireman*. Reading, MA: Addison-Wesley, 1952. (PS-2).

Bundt, Nancy. *The Fire Station Book*. Minneapolis, MN: Carolrhoda, 1981. (PS-3).

Cameron, Elizabeth. *The Big Book of Real Fire Engines*. New York: Putnam, 1973. (2-7).

Gergely, Tibor. *The Great Big Fire Engine Book*. New York: Western, 1950. (K-2).

Gibbons, Gail. *The Post Office Book*. New York: Harper & Row, 1982. (K-3).

Keats, Ezra. *Letter to Amy*. New York: Harper & Row, 1968. (K-3).

Krementz, Jill. *Taryn Goes to the Dentist*. New York: Crown, 1986. (2-4).

Rey, Margaret. *Curious George at the Fire Station*. Boston: Houghton Mifflin, 1985. (K-3).

Robinson, Barry, and Martin J. Dain. *On the Beat, Policemen at Work*. New York: Harcourt Brace Jovanovich, 1968. (2-4).

STUDENT WORKSHEETS

Community-Helper Worksheet 1

Name _____

Listen for directions.

Skills: following verbal directions, visual discrimination, fine motor (drawing and coloring)

Community-Helper Worksheet 2

Name _____

Find the things a police officer uses. Color them.

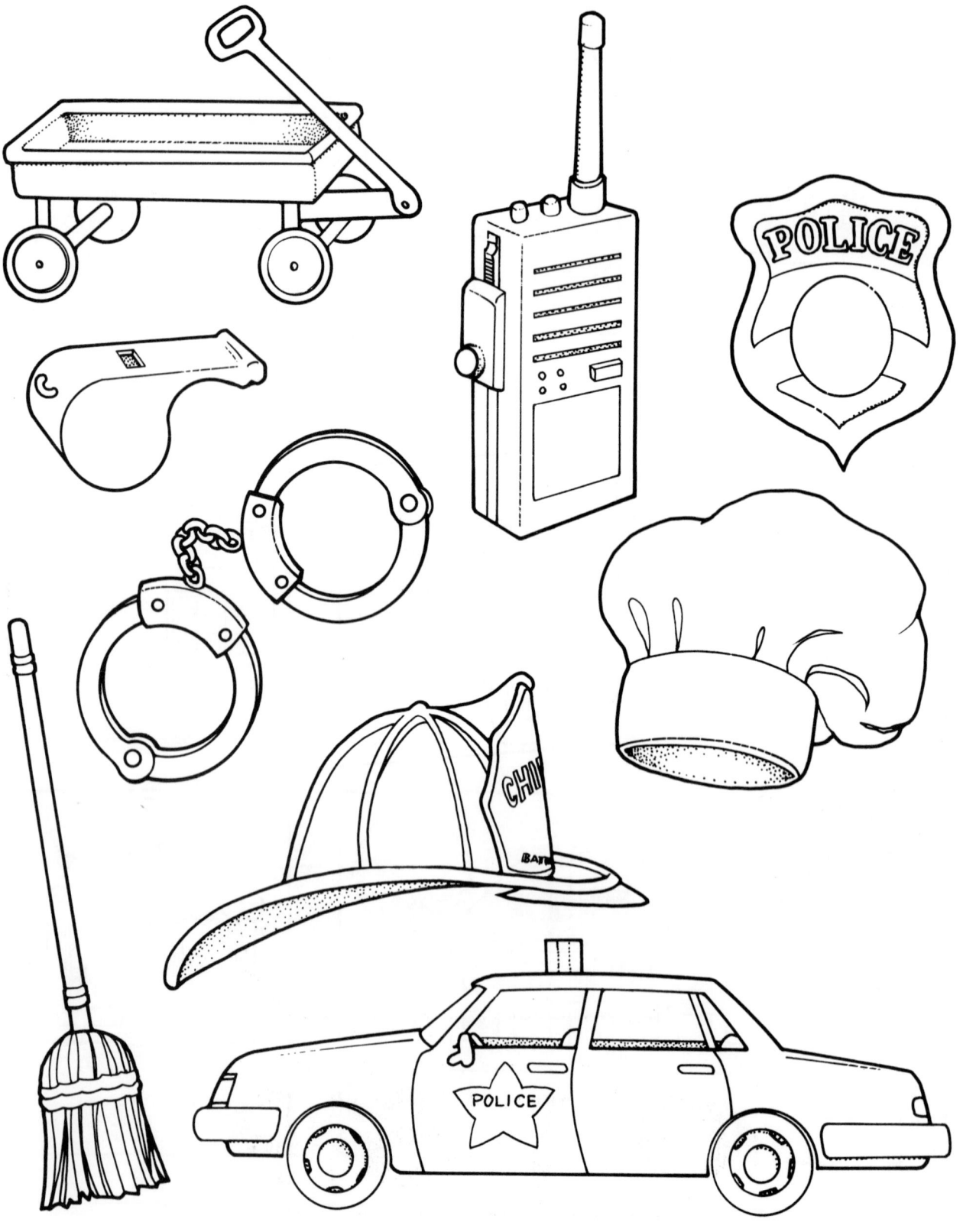

20 Skills: visual discrimination, fine motor (coloring)

Community-Helper Worksheet 3

Name _____

Color the stop sign red. Cut and then paste the letters to make the word *stop*.

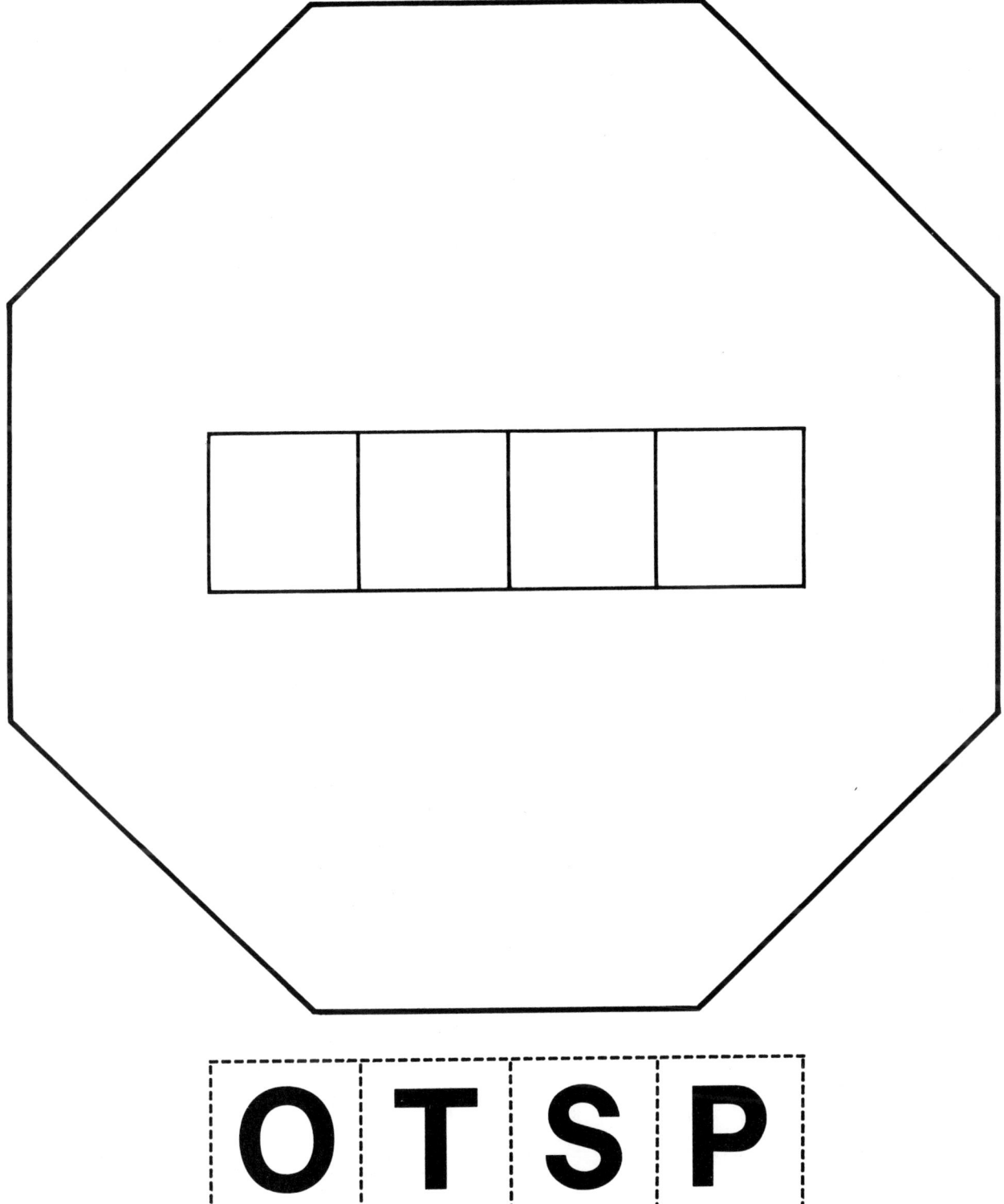

Skills: former simple words, fine motor (coloring, cutting, and pasting) 21

Community-Helper Worksheet 4

Name _____

Color the spaces these colors:

1=red   3=brown

2=yellow   4=green

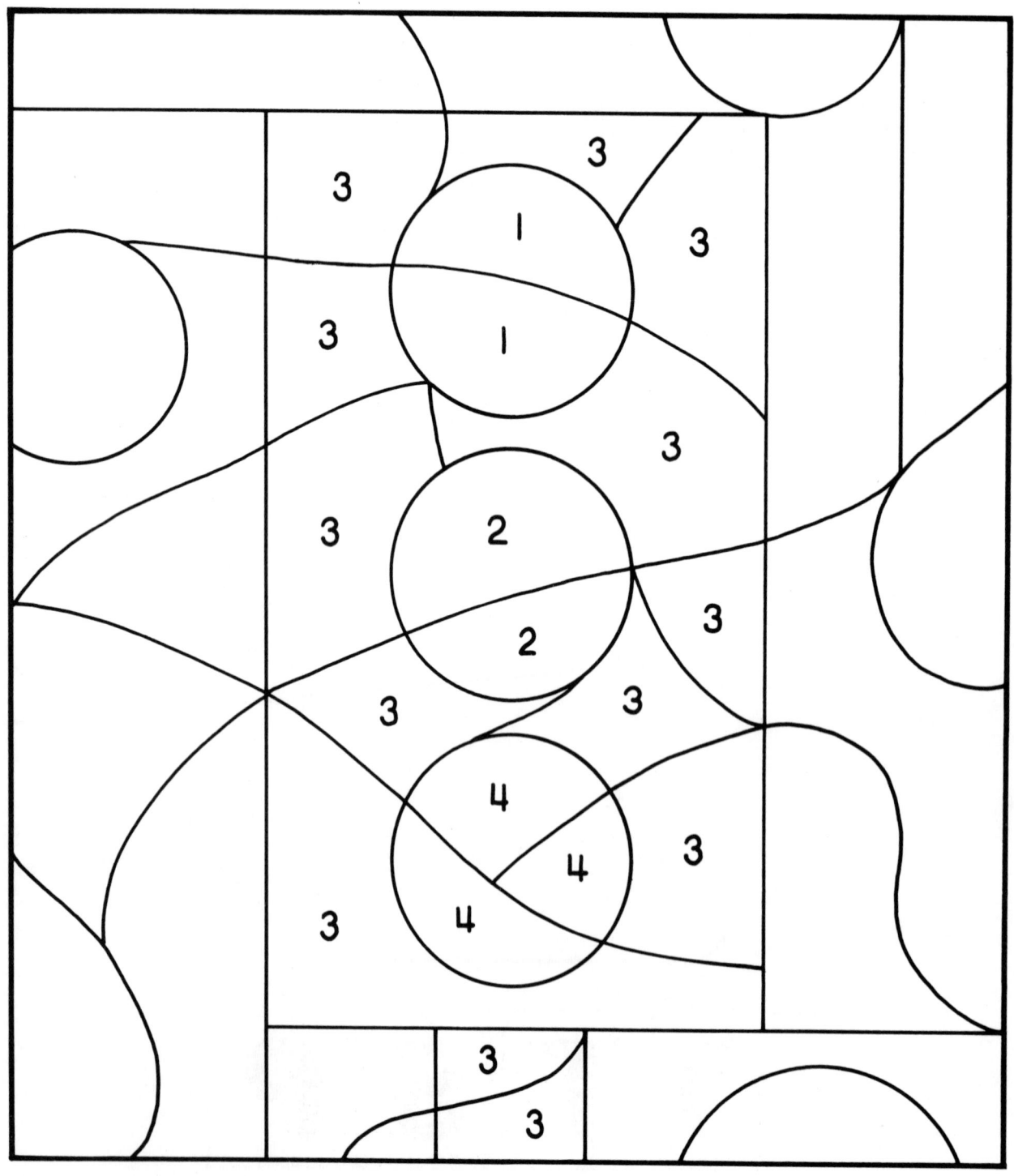

22   Skills: number and color recognition, fine motor (coloring)

Community-Helper Worksheet 5

Name _____

Look at each row. Find the pattern. Cut and then paste the picture that completes the pattern.

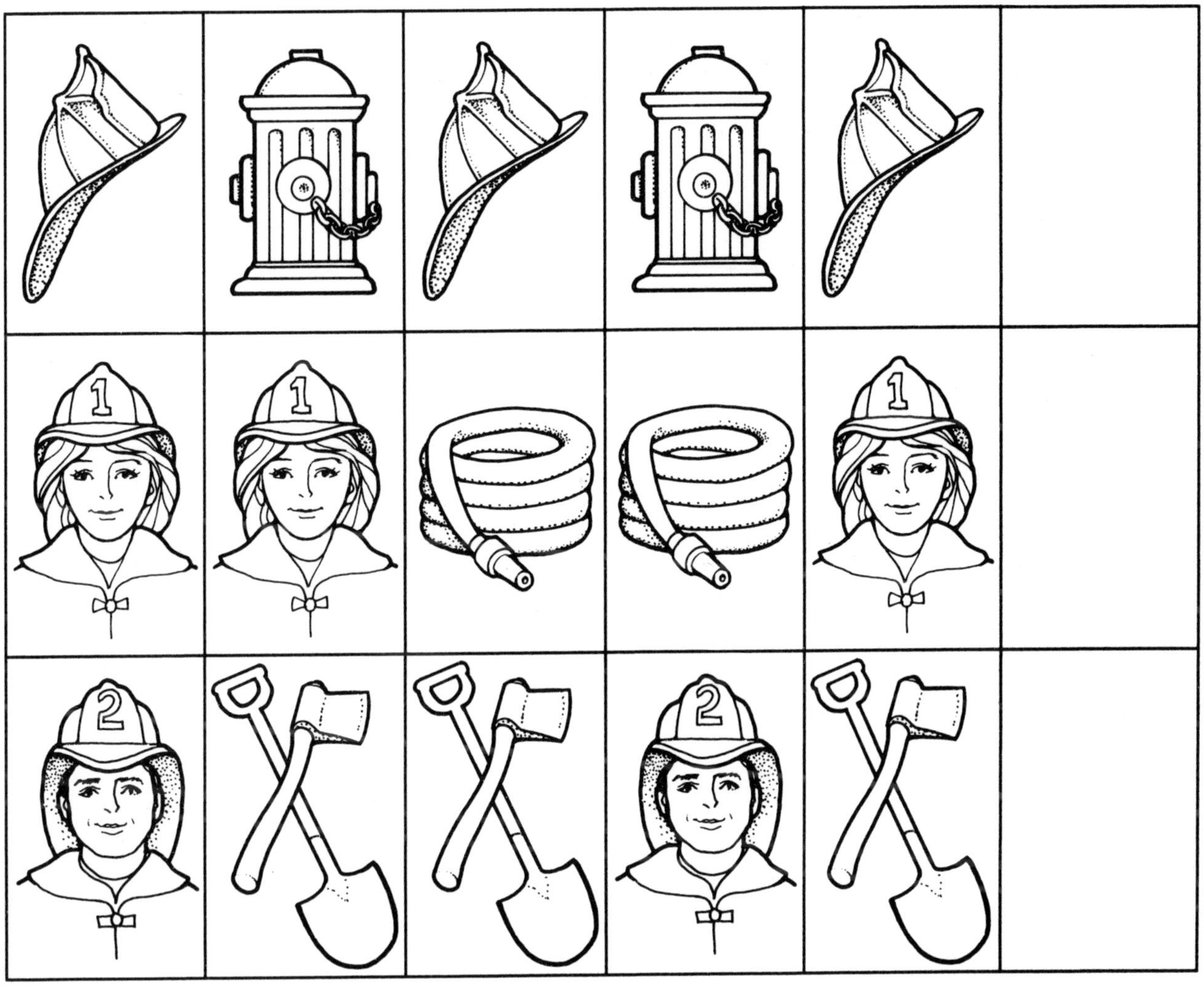

Skills: sequencing, visual discrimination, fine motor (cutting and pasting)

Community-Helper Worksheet 6

Name _____

Connect the dots in order from 1 to 25.

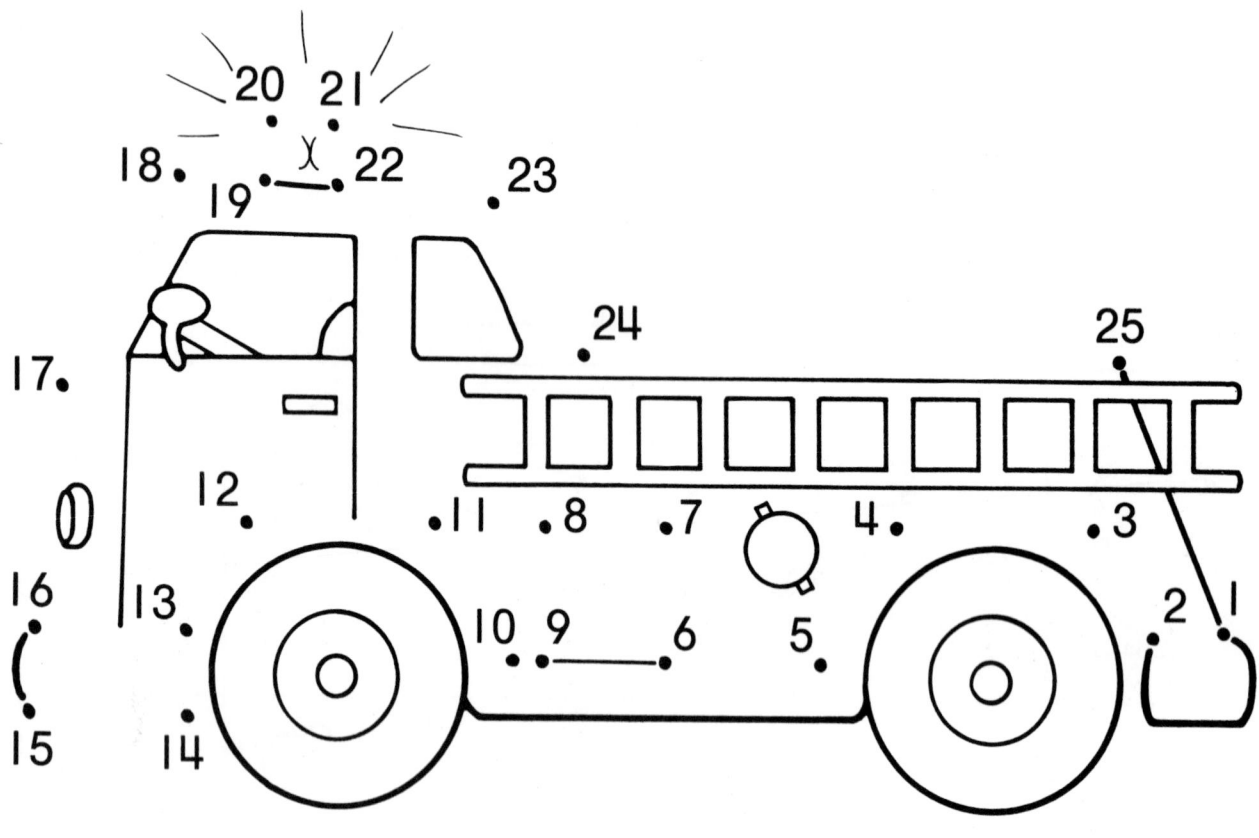

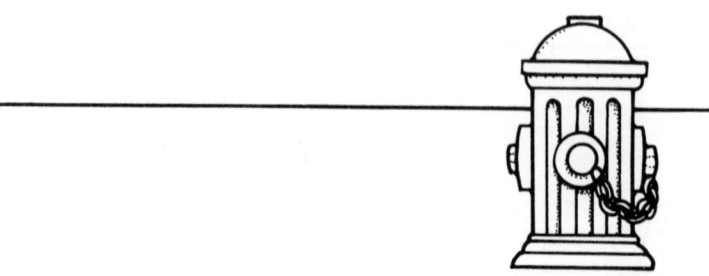

24 Skills: counting to 25, fine motor (drawing)

Community-Helper Worksheet 7

Name _____

In each row, find the objects that match. Color them the same.

Skills: understanding concept of *same*, visual discrimination, fine motor (coloring)

Community-Helper Worksheet 8

Name _____

Cut and then paste the cards in order to tell a story.

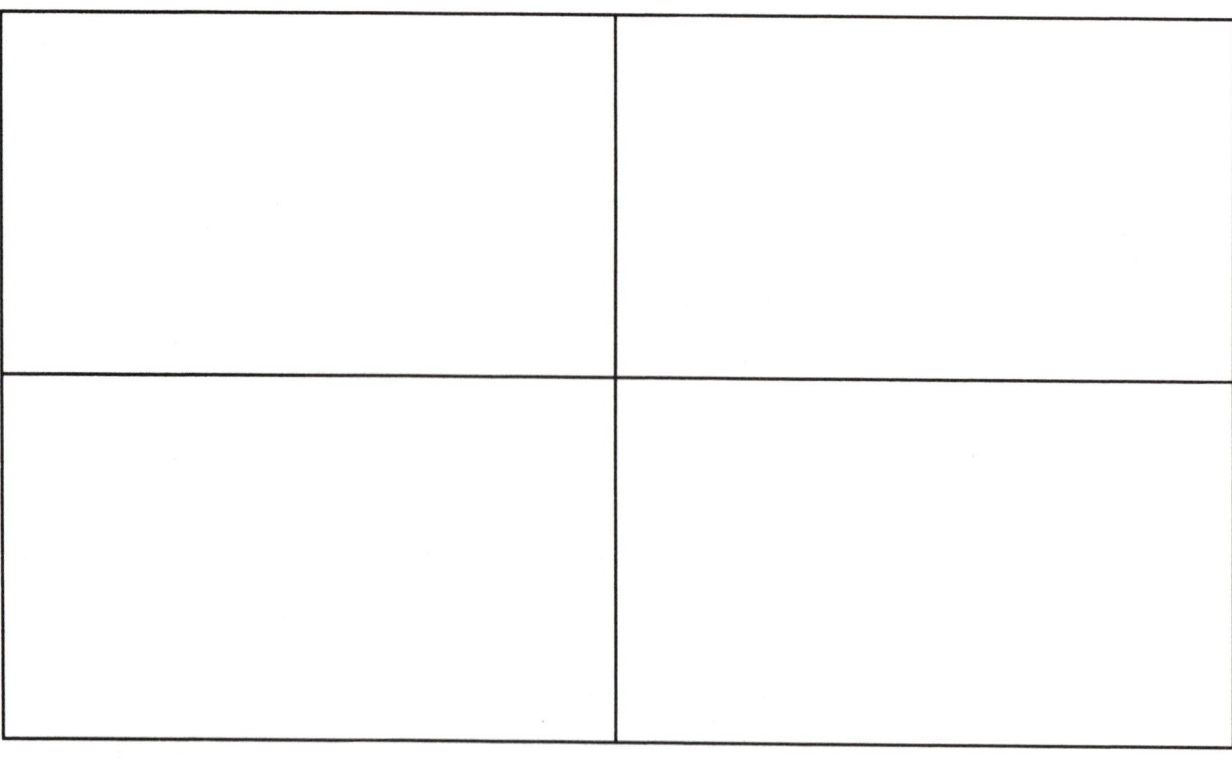

Community-Helper Worksheet 9

Name _____

Help the fire truck find the burning house. Do not cross any lines.

Skills: fine motor (drawing)

Community-Helper Worksheet 10

Name _____

Connect the dots in order from A to Z.

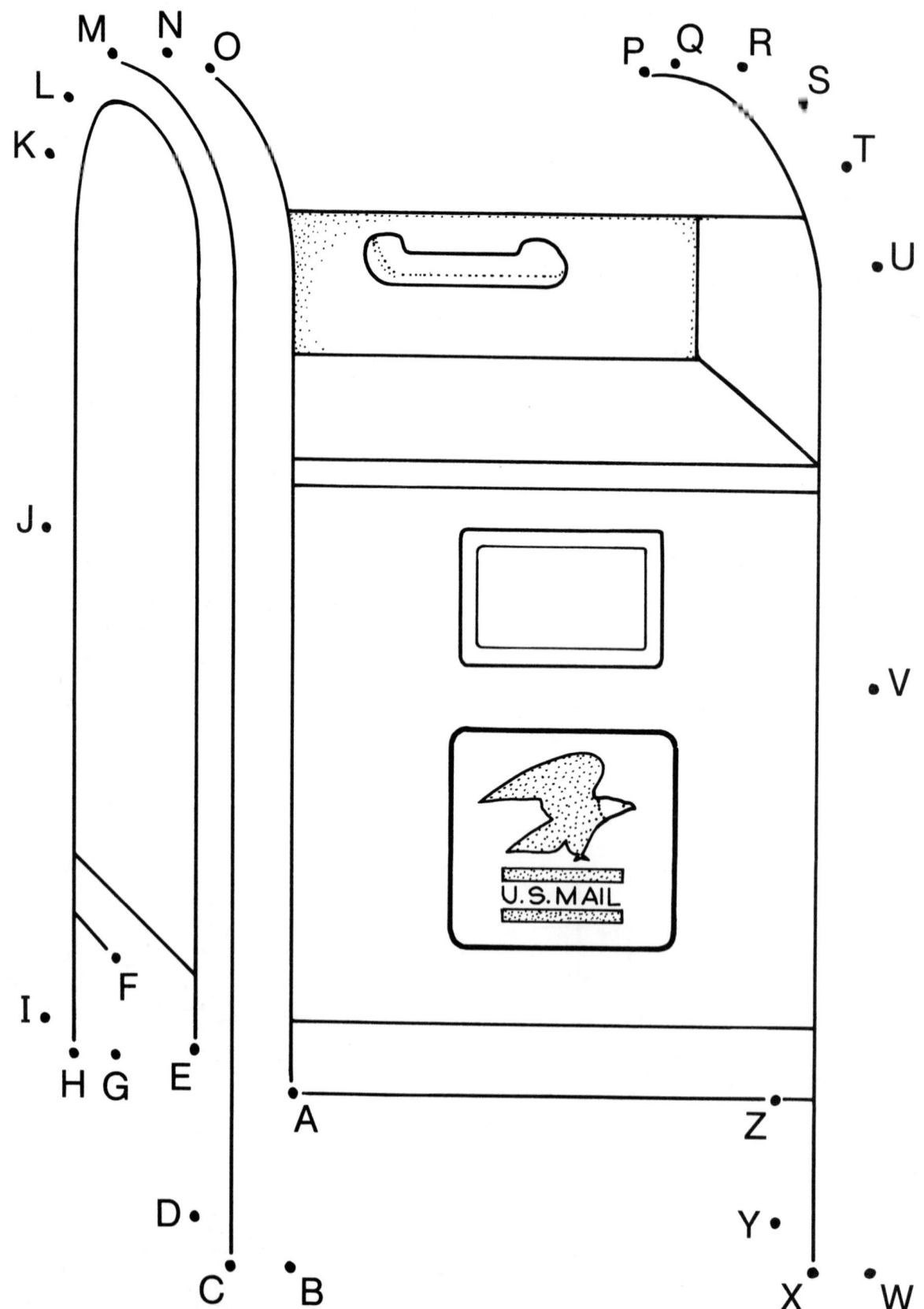

28   Skills: alphabetizing letters, fine motor (drawing)

Community-Helper Worksheet 11

Name _____

Help each community helper get to his or her vehicle. Trace each dotted line without lifting your pencil.

Skills: fine motor (drawing)

Community-Helper Worksheet 12

Name _____

Cut out the tool cards.
Paste each tool next to the helper who uses the tool.

police officer

fire fighter

letter carrier

teacher

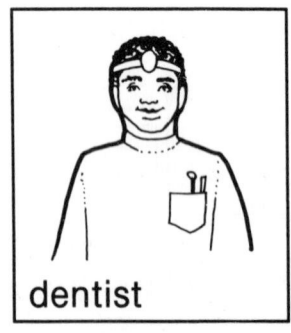
dentist

baker

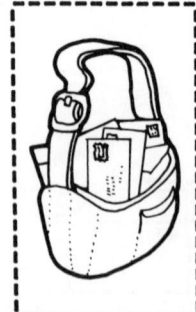  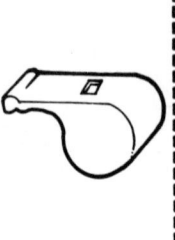  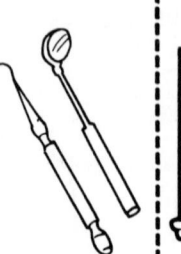 

30   Skills: visual discrimination, fine motor (cutting and pasting)

Community-Helper Worksheet 13

Name _____

In each row, find the objects that match. Color them the same.

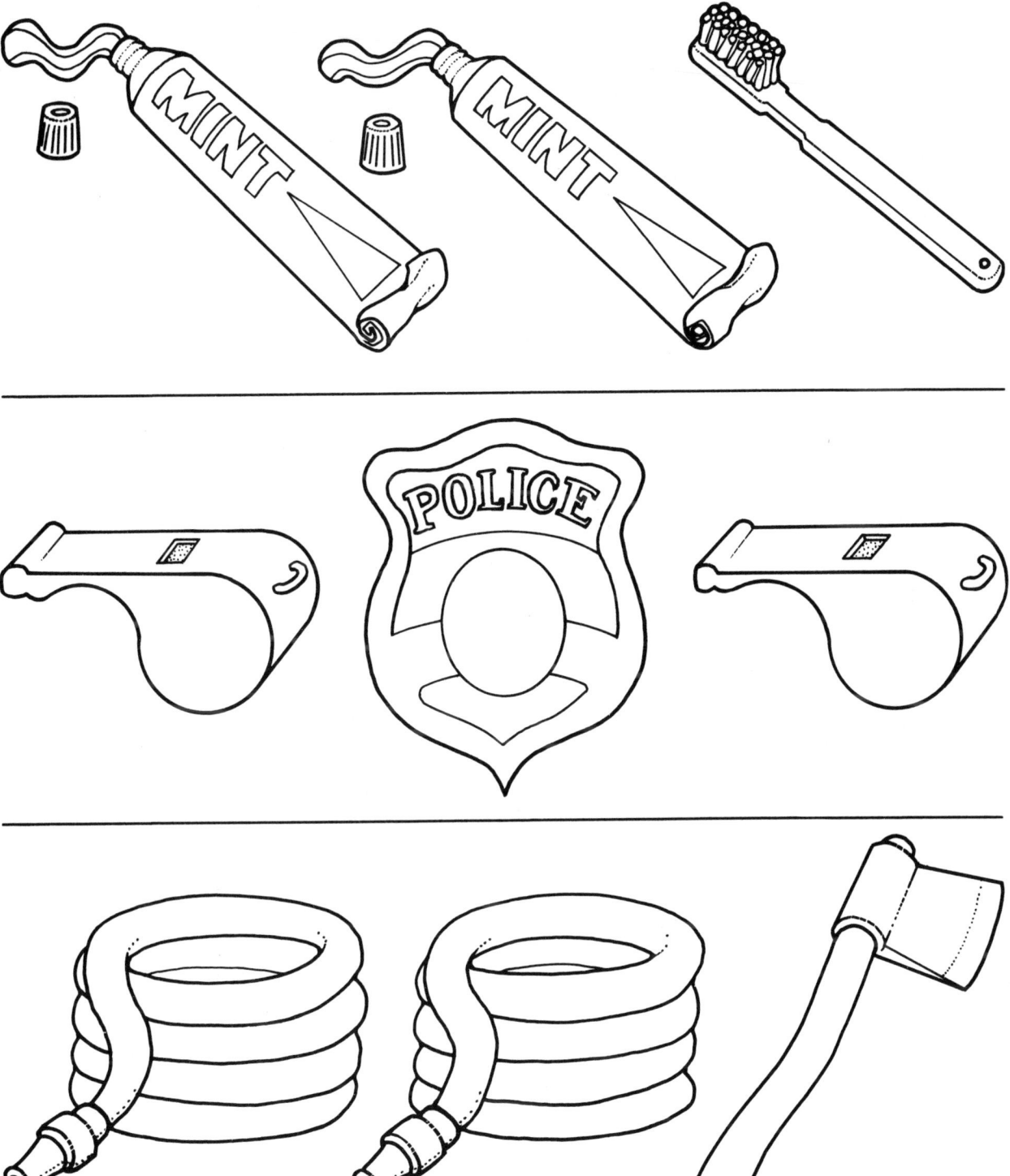

Skills: understanding concept of *same*, visual discrimination, fine motor (coloring)   31

Community-Helper Worksheet 14

Name _____

In each row, find the helper picture that is different. Circle it. Color the pictures.

32 Skills: understanding concept of *different*, visual discrimination, fine motor (drawing and coloring)

PATTERN PAGES

Community-Helper Book Patterns

police officer

35

Community-Helper Book Patterns

fire fighter

Community-Helper Book Patterns

dentist

37

Community-Helper Book Patterns

letter carrier

Community-Helper Book Patterns

doctor

39

Community-Helper Book Patterns

teacher

Community-Helper Patterns

41

Community-Helper Patterns

42

We Learn All About Community Helpers, © 1988

Community-Helper Patterns

43